ayahuasca!

(or not)

for Linda

ayahuasca!
(or not)

Russell Helms

Disappointed after his mortgage fell through, Daniel decided to take a trip. He only made $34K per year teaching English at the local college, and expenses always outlasted his income, but he had saved for the down payment for the failed mortgage with extra income from his editing business. His rent crested at over $1,000 per month, half of his take-home pay. He had downgraded his internet connection and canceled his cable to cut costs. True, his taste for cigars kept cash slim, but he had reduced his intake of bourbon from a handle every ten days to just a drink or so per week. He'd bought a cheap bottle of Evan Williams, and the paintlike essence did not please his taste buds and had turned him off to bourbon in general. He could have pushed the bottle to the back of the cabinet and moved on, but felt that he had to finish the nearly two liters out of duty.

Daniel fit the bill of a typical English professor. He was tall, quiet, with thinning black hair. He tended to talk slowly and carefully, with just a hint of a Southern accent. At fifty-three, he was only an instructor and not a professor, having spent the first twenty years of his professional career in healthcare. But, no matter, he enjoyed his academic career and did not lust after the big bucks that being a hospital administrator would have brought him. He was content with his life, two years beyond an amicable divorce, and actively involved with his two daughters.

Having been raised in a strict Southern Baptist home, Daniel had not tasted alcohol until he was thirty while in graduate school. There had been so many things that he had not tasted or tried, and, as in his career, he felt that he was twenty years behind in enjoying the pleasures of life, thus, the cigars and bourbon. He'd smoked pot a few times, but received little pleasure from it, other than the pleasant smell. And at the age of fifty-three, he was ready and willing to explore the wider world, the curious world, the exotic and forbidden. Thus, his desire to visit Peru, a center of ayahuasca healing, a place to blow one's mind and see the demons within.

Daniel had also considered heroin as an object of desire, but it was illegal in most countries, and he worried about becoming addicted. He could barely afford mid-range cigars. Cocaine, crack, and meth were not attractive, being too heavy on the chemicals required to make them. Peyote was of interest, but it was the DMT in ayahuasca that called to him from the jungle. The drug was even touted as being a cure for depression, which Daniel had in spades.

It was a Monday. Daniel had walked his mutt Stella, fed the cats, and cleaned the litterbox. It was summer, and he only had one online class, scientific writing, which had ended just a few days prior. After a dinner of five greasy fish filets from the oven and loads of ketchup, he sat down with the idea of settling his desire for adventure with an internet search. He read stories warning travelers of the potentially fatal aspects of ayahuasca, especially in regard to interaction with antidepressants, which he took, again, in spades, and without which he was fairly dysfunctional. In his mind, he merely decided that he would just go off his meds a few days prior and all would be well, even though attempts in the past had brought him to the edge of despair.

He read of rapes during the ceremonies, of unscrupulous shamans, and the side effects of ayahuasca, which involved tedious vomiting and possibly soiling oneself. The DMT was actually in the chacruna plant and was readily metabolized by the human body, rendering it ineffective, but the ancient Amazonians had found a way to trick the body into absorbing the hallucinogen by combining it with the mysterious ayahuasca vine—the vine of the soul. The cost of this cocktail was the puking, but the reward was the hallucinogenic experience, or so he gathered.

A center of the ayahuasca ritual seemed to be located around the city of Iquitos, Peru. Several organizations touted their services in the form of week-long retreats, usually with four or five ayahuasca ceremonies included. Most of the retreats focused on the drug's spiritual aspects and included activities such as yoga, mindful painting, and fruit-and-mud body scrubs. This did not appeal to Daniel, but it seemed that he would have to bear some psychic discomfort to enjoy the healing experience. Within thirty minutes, he had chosen a retreat called Pitarika, which did not mention yoga or use the term "mindfulness." Within another ten minutes, he had registered, lied about taking antidepressants, and charged $800 to his credit card. Game on.

The next day, he dropped by his ex-wife's house, where his two daughters, Chelsea and Samantha, lived. Chelsea was sixteen and almost as tall as he was. She was sweet sixteen and working part-time at an ice cream shop. She'd thought she would skip college, but dipping ice cream had changed her tune. Samantha was a year younger than Chelsea. She was the extrovert of the two and could talk for hours with her friends. She couldn't wait for college, much to Chelsea's chagrin. Daniel grilled burgers and told them about his trip, planned for the end of July. He would fly into Iquitos from Lima, have two days in Iquitos before the retreat, and two days after the retreat. No one was really surprised by his bold announcement, but worried that he would come to an ill fate, tripping in the jungle.

Daniel mollified them, saying that the ceremonies were monitored by watchers who made sure that no one got hurt. Remy, his ex-wife, worried that he would be drugged and robbed and possibly shot in the head. Remy was a pistol, a dean at the college where he taught. She made four times his salary and had developed into quite the administrator, dealing with the craziness of academia. Her shoulder-length hair was streaked with gray, and she was the shortest of the group. Remy's comment about being shot in the head made Daniel laugh, although he had contemplated the same thing. He made the mistake of telling them about the interactions between the ayahuasca and his antidepressants, and they all agreed that he was crazy and that he should not go. He just laughed and assured them that he would go off his meds beforehand and that all would be fine. So, Remy had asked, you're going to go off your meds while we're in Florida? They had all planned to visit a friend on St. George Island, an annual trip to the beach. Daniel reassured them that he would be fine, that their trip to Florida wasn't in danger.

Meanwhile, he had to prepare for his trip to Peru, and using money he would have used as a down payment on a house, he ordered nice things: an Osprey backpack, Boggs half-boots, synthetic shirts and shorts from REI, a new Dell mini-laptop, and then necessities such as bug spray, socks, and ear buds for his phone. His passport had expired, and he sent his application, choosing the express option. The passport photo, he took with his laptop. He thought he looked a bit moon-faced and wondered whether he really did.

There was a month to go before the trip, and he did normal things: editing his epic novel series set in Nigeria, writing short stories, sending out stories for publication, and prepping for his fall classes. He had just purchased a new bike—a nice one, a matte-black Kona Honzo—and rode every day, building up his stamina. Back in the day, he had ridden his mountain bike to work and tooled around on weekends. On his second outing with the new bike, he stopped going up a steep hill and fell over, his feet clipped to the pedals. He landed on the point of his elbow, blood squirting.

The family trip to Florida soon rolled around, and Daniel began to anticipate his trip to Peru, which would follow, for real. The Florida adventure was the

designated time when he would stop his meds cold tur-
key: an antidepressant (of which he took the maximum
dosage), an antipsychotic (for his suicidal thoughts),
and an amphetamine (to boost his antidepressant). The
retreat brochure had stated that all psychiatric meds
should be discontinued five to seven weeks before im-
bibing ayahuasca, but he figured five days would suffice.

He stopped the meds the day before driving down
to St. George and felt it. It was a vague yawn in his
head, asking, Where's the drugs, man? What's up? The
drive took ten hours, and he was thoroughly whipped,
feeling like he'd been sitting on a riding lawn mower
and it was still moving. Their friend, who owned the
beach house, Maddy, welcomed them with open arms.
She was seventy with bushy white hair combed down.
She smoked like a chimney and had recently lost her
husband, Freddie. They had been such a pair, and she
was still in shock. Being on the island, it had taken
paramedics thirty minutes to arrive, but too late. The
house just didn't feel complete without Freddie and his
dry wit.

The beach house was actually not on the beach, but
on the bay side of the island. The house was well-worn,
having survived several hurricanes. One thing Daniel liked about the house was that there was no paint
or stain, just natural wood. Maddy's outside feral cat
population had dropped from its heyday of twenty or
so to just four, plus the three inside cats. Every day, she
bought fresh shrimp and fed them to the cats in addi-
tion to wet cat food. Feeding the cats twice a day was a

religious practice for her.

The four visitors reigned over the bottom floor, which was serviced by one window air conditioner. Samantha took the room with Daniel, and Chelsea with Remy. It was nearly midnight when they arrived, and everyone pretty much tanked and went to bed. Daniel couldn't sleep, at first, but the next morning could not wake up. Remy let him sleep in till two. When he awoke, he was so groggy, and his eyes felt like there was a board between them. He staggered up the stairs, practicing making his mouth move. Maddy and Remy were sitting at the square island at the head of the stairs and watched him hesitate. Samantha pulled up a chair and asked if he was okay.

Words tried to come from his mouth, but stuck to his tongue. He eventually said, How's Everyone? But it came out like hardening glue. Remy said that he looked terrible, and Samantha just laughed. Daniel could feel the molasses inside his head, his eyes darting, as if trying to escape one another, accompanied by flashes of being off balance. Everyone had a good short laugh, and soon the topic of being off his meds and going to Peru cropped up. Remy said that there was no way he could function, no way he could navigate his way to Peru if he were as fucked up as he was now. Maddy was on board with Remy and had printed out a couple of articles that played the downsides of the ayahuasca industry.

Daniel just avoided talking and downed a glass of fresh-squeezed orange juice. There were also waffles and bacon left over from breakfast, and, after getting coffee, he dug in, hoping the food would jolt him into normalcy, but nothing happened except that he was compelled to sleep, which he did until seven, waking up in time for stir-fry à la Maddy. Daniel felt awful. He was gazing into the abyss, feeling despair, and beginning to doubt his ability to travel. After dinner, he went promptly back to bed and dreamed chaotic dreams of dentist's offices made of cement with long, narrow staircases.

The prior day, Daniel had missed out on beach time with the girls. But he hadn't even brought a bathing suit, hoping really to avoid the beach altogether. He'd had one melanoma removed from his chest and hated putting on sunscreen anyway. He pried himself out of bed, hearing Remy and Maddy chatting at the top of the stairs. He felt absolutely crazy. Destructive thoughts filled his head: hanging, shooting, drowning. He would just walk into the ocean and inhale the water. He was exhausted.

Daniel said, Hey, and Maddy was making omelets. He said to make his small and with a bit of cheese. There was bacon, and he ate a piece. Remy had taught Maddy how to bake the bacon in the oven, rendering it crisp and flat. The oven temperature needed was 475 degrees, and Daniel always worried that it was too high, that the bacon grease would catch on fire. It occurred to him that he never fantasized about dying in a fire. That was something.

Increasingly, the conversation hinged on the upcoming trip to Peru, everyone chipping away at his rebuttals that he would be fine. But he was slipping into oblivion and knew that he would never be able to pack his backpack, let alone navigate an airport. Unable to take his withdrawal any longer, he caved and took his pills and slept. It took until later that night, but he was feeling a bit better and re-thinking his plans for a drug-crazed jungle trip. He looked at the clock, and it was ten. They had all watched a movie together, *Fahrenheit 9/11,* and he'd begun to get angry at the stupidity of it all, at the power of money, at the baldness of the lies, of the public's ignorance. Osama bin Laden, trained to fight in the United States, was practically Bush's god-son. He went to bed and, lying there, decided to cancel his trip. He had plenty of work that needed attention, plus he was feeling guilty about having a sitter come to see about the cats, Checkers and Chess. Stella was to stay at Remy's house.

Chelsea was in her bed, headphones on, watching YouTube videos. Daniel turned, got her attention, and told her that he was not going to Peru. Saying it washed relief over him. He wouldn't have to cram on his Spanish. He wouldn't have to deal with the five-hour layover in Newark, the eight-hour layover in Lima. He could just work and ride his bike every day. The cats and Stella would be happier. Everything would be normal. Canceling the trip seemed the right thing to do. Chelsea nodded and said that it was his decision.

The next day, everyone knew that Daniel had caved. Chelsea had broken the news. There were congrats all around. Daniel was back to feeling normal and up at a decent hour, before noon. Breakfast was French toast and the flat perfectly cooked bacon. After his brunch, Daniel got to work canceling his trip, hoping to get his money back or at least receive credits. First, he emailed the retreat, Pitarika, and asked that his reservation be canceled and any monies refunded. Next—he dreaded it—he tackled the flights and hotel in Iquitos, which he had booked through Orbitz. He had purchased their vacation protection package. Surely, all was well.

He first went to the website and found the instructions on how to change or cancel a flight. It said there would be a Modify button once he clicked on the itinerary. Once there, though, the Modify space was blank, nothing to click on. He tried a different browser—nothing —and then, his worst fear: he had to call, which he hated. A man with a strong Indian accent answered. He said that it would cost $300 to cancel the flight. What the hell? Daniel just told him to forget it. He just wouldn't show up and eat the $1500 in airfare. It was a sunk cost, right? Gone, no matter if he went or stayed. Meanwhile, he received an email from Pitarika. It was too late to refund his money, but he would have a credit with them for a future visit. Hey, no problem!

The last day of the visit came, and it was bagels and prosciutto for breakfast with cream cheese. Daniel had avoided going to the beach entirely, a minor miracle. By now, taking his pills, his mind was clear once again, and he began to doubt canceling the retreat. They said their goodbyes to Maddy around noon, drove across the causeway, and stopped to buy gas. Daniel discovered that he'd left his wallet at Maddy's and then had to drive back to fetch it. The drive was long enough without stupidity like that.

Daniel drove the entire way back, shifting from one hip to another. He thought about his decision to cancel Peru and felt that it had been a rash decision made in his withdrawal delirium under pressure from the family and Maddy. He couldn't just let the whole deal slip through his fingers. He'd already posted on Facebook that he was going, and several people had replied that they wanted to hear about his experience. He couldn't disappoint the fans, could he? Should he just go and hang out in Iquitos, perhaps take a jungle tour? He wondered if he could do an ayahuasca experience in the city itself. But that seemed second-rate to a jungle experience. He mulled it over and over. He would have one more day to decide before the scheduled flight. There would be lots to do: packing, paying the rent, buying more cat litter, lining up the sitter for the cats.

That night, having gotten in around ten, Daniel took an excited Stella back to the apartment and thoroughly rubbed and scratched the cats, who seemed perplexed that he had actually returned. Onto his laptop he went, searching for some sort of compromise to salvage his trip. After a few websites, he hit gold, a jungle tour outfit that included a single ayahuasca ceremony on a three-day, two-night tour south of Iquitos. He would just have to ignore the warnings about not taking the meds and risk it. He would not take them, perhaps the day before and the day of. That seemed reasonable. And he could sip his ceremonial tea slowly, in moderation. He would vomit a few times and visit with himself inside his crowded head. Perfect, and he hit the Buy Now button, $342. To reward himself for his forward action, he took a cigar, a Nica Puro, out on the patio and edited a novel for about forty-five minutes, puffing and deleting unnecessary words such as "up" after "stood."

The next day, he awoke late, around two. The meds had righted his being, but he was back in the pattern of sleeping too late. Upon opening his eyes in the morning, all seemed lost, and all he could do was clench his eyes and crave just another ten minutes of sleep, hitting snooze over and over and over. Usually, the only way he could get up was in response to a bladder bursting with fat pee. He would stumble to the toilet, banging his shoulders against the doorframes. Then, he just had to make it into the kitchen and warm up a cup of coffee. Next, he would take his meds, always with juice. Upon his leaving the bed, Stella would stretch and yip, jump down, and stand beside the sliding glass door to the patio. Seeing Daniel slip on shoes, she would woof, encouraging him to hurry up.

The air was warm and solid like the inside of a beating heart. Stella lunged, pulling Daniel onto the patio, jamming her nose into the grass, squatting to pee. Daniel stumbled into the sunshine, rubbing his eyes, yawning, still feeling hopeless, but at least he was up. Down the steep hill they went, Daniel slipping, and onto the quiet road behind the complex. The walk lasted fifteen minutes or so, a circle back to the patio. Once inside, there was more coffee, and then he was tilted back in his beat-up recliner. Stella liked to dig into the seat, ripping the vinyl covering.

Reclined, he inhaled with his eyes closed, fighting the negative thoughts. There were always the fleeting glimpses of suicide, of a trip to the gun store, even on the meds, but at least they did not nag at him hour after hour for days on end until he was too exhausted to breathe. The recliner was kind of like going back to bed, but not quite. One step closer to normalcy. Without classes to tend to, he could afford to "relax" in the recliner for one or two hours, which passed by in a rush. He'd just finished a book project, but needed to do some work on an Institutional Review Board (IRB) proposal.

And so, after an hour in the recliner, Stella on the couch with her nose on her paws, Daniel lured himself outside onto the patio with a cigar and the need to get the IRB proposal right. After two hours of crockpotting in the ninety-degree heat, shirt damp, forehead beaded, cigar gone, all felt right with the world, and the despair of the morning seemed a distant dream, although it would return the next morning like clockwork. Back inside the cooler apartment, the phone rang, and it was Remy asking what he had decided to do about Peru. He briefly told her about the jungle tour, but left out the part about the ayahuasca ceremony. There had been much joy on St. George Island when he'd announced that he was canceling the retreat.

So, now, instead of seven days of relative inactivity in the jungle, he would have a three-day jungle trek, plus one ayahuasca ceremony. The rest of the time would be spent in Iquitos. She was grilling chicken that night, and since he was leaving early the next morning, he came over to fill in Remy and the girls on his new plan. In his mind, he had salvaged the trip and reached a truce, a compromise. The only thing that worried him was the interaction between his meds and the ayahuasca.

The grilled chicken was pretty good; the Brussels sprouts scorched in an iron skillet were even better. Chelsea made Caprese salad, and there were strawberries with whipped cream for dessert. "What's my favorite color?" And Samantha went through her litany of questions, very upbeat, and not sad when Daniel couldn't remember her favorite movie. Meanwhile, Remy had moved on to more practical matters, such as upcoming school fees. Since Remy was buying all of the girls' school clothes, she suggested that Daniel cover the school fees, and he mumbled an affirmative.

It was about nine, and time to leave. He had brought Stella to stay with them, and he gave her a full belly rub. She did her little smile, showing her top teeth. He called them her corn teeth. He had to run by Walmart for a poncho and cat litter. While there, he managed a few more items, including a Roku stick so that he could watch Netflix on his TV. Fifty bucks. He remembered he needed sheets. After falling on his mountain bike, he had bled all over his sheets from the

hole in his elbow. That was another fifty bucks. He had
a hankering for ice cream and dropped a pint of Ben
and Jerry's chocolate brownie in the basket. Back home,
he packed his backpack, wrote his rent check, and
watched three episodes of *Forensic Files,* while eating ice
cream. He gave the cats extra love, knowing he would
be gone for eleven days, but Checkers, the white male,
was being a bad kitty, knocking shit off of high places,
including a can of diet ginger ale.

Daniel decided it was pointless to go to bed and
so coaxed himself outside with a cigar to do some
novel editing. It was warm like pudding, and his feet
felt like they were inside hotdog buns. He kicked off
his tennis shoes and pecked on his backlit keyboard.
Cicadas chattered in chorus, rival groups outsinging
one another. It was his second cigar of the day, and his
upper lip on the inside had begun to peel, the tobacco
and heat stinging the flesh. His wounded elbow had
stopped bleeding, and the hole had filled in somewhat,
but there was a small bag of fluid that had gathered
there, squishy to the touch. He was worried about a
sterile abscess and couldn't help pressing the bulge like
it would pop.

The end of the cigar signaled the end of the out-
door session, and inside he went to finish packing and
charging his phone and the cute little Dell computer
he had bought, leaving his sacred Macbook at home,
hidden in a drawer. Three-thirty and all was well,
it seemed, and so he had earned another episode of
Forensic Files. His flight left at 6:15 a.m., and before he

knew it, it was 4:45. He hurried, showered, shoved his rent check into a dropbox, and sped off down the road toward the airport twenty minutes away. He arrived at 5:45 and was soon at the gate, with time to grab a piping hot coffee, of which he drank half before tossing it, worried it would make him pee. His flight was direct to Newark, where he had a five-hour layover.

Day One

Newark proved tolerable, but he had heartburn. He ate a cold chicken salad wrap and drank a fruit smoothie, which helped a bit. At his terminal, there were lots of what he assumed to be Peruvians headed to Lima with a scattering of gringos. In his back pocket, he had a list of Spanish phrases printed out, including conjugations of ser and estar and how to ask for a salon de tatuaje, in case he had time for a tattoo. It was real. He was going. At this point, the ayahuasca seemed a moot point, but still lingered in his mind, kind of like a cartoon. While he waited, he began writing a novella about a guy who goes to Peru to hallucinate in the jungle. The protagonist originally had booked a week-long retreat, but while going off his meds to prepare for the experience, he decided to not go, but then, after resuming his pills, had come to a compromise: a jungle tour with a single ayahuasca experience.

Before boarding, Daniel had a coffee, a grande Pike no cream, bringing back the heartburn. Once on board, he passed through first class, which was always amusing. He imagined that he was walking down an aisle of kennels at the local animal shelter, that the first-class passengers were homeless dogs, but with their own private bathroom. In economy, he snagged the aisle seat, a bonus, and had beside him a skinny kid, giving everybody plenty of room. The flight was epic—eight hours, four thousand miles—and he started it off reading a book for the PhD program he had just been admitted to at the college where he taught. The book, right away, shocked him as poorly written, kind of slapped together, even though it was the fourth edition. There was talk of the importance of listening to others, of exploring one's thoughts and experiences through descriptive narrative, how the experience was enlightening, and so on. The poorly integrated quotes really leaped out and grabbed him. This was a C paper at best, if he had been grading. Disappointed, he turned to a reading for a class he was teaching in the fall on the Ethiopian Famine of 1983–86. A piece about the politics of celebrity and humanitarian aid.

By then, he was pretty sleepy and absolutely cold. The flight information screen on the back of the seat in front of him noted that it was negative 65 outside at 21,000 feet. Fucking cold and high. He pulled the thin blanket around his shoulders and closed his eyes, not sure if he actually slept or just dozed, as if with a nasty flu and saturated with cold medicine. He shifted, bent his knees, rubbed the bulb of fluid on his elbow, and then had to pee, a blessing to be in the aisle seat.

Reading and writing. Daniel's protagonist was on

a plane to Lima, Peru, writing about a man traveling to Peru to visit the city of Iquitos, to do a little jungle tour, and to have an ayahuasca experience, perhaps receiving at least enlightenment but maybe even a cure for depression. The protagonist's feet felt like they were inside hot dog buns.

Daniel read more from the fourth edition book, which he would have graded as a C. He wondered if it was a joke. Really? What the hell? He could barely stand the prose, rambling and pasted together with poorly integrated quotes. He wanted to break the oval window and toss the book from on high, but that seemed far-fetched, but perhaps not for his protagonist. Maybe he would add that detail, sending the plane down in flames in the Amazon.

Dinner was served, chicken or pasta, and he chose the pasta. It must have been a cheese ravioli, and tasted fair. No complaints. There was some sort of grain salad with cranberries that was odd, but he ate it, feeling the power of fiber. He sat back, enthralled with the possibilities for his protagonist. Would he kill him off? Perhaps let his meds make a deadly cocktail with the ayahuasca? Should he set it up as a kind of suicide, with the reader grieving for him, or perhaps as an accidental overdose scenario, the unlikable victim deserving of his punishment? But the protagonist had to be likable. No one likes to read about an asshole experiencing serendipity and winning the lottery.

A final sleep, and then it was wide awake with reluctant reading for the last half hour, the plane slicing into Lima like a lime into tequila. Bumpity bump, whoosh, and all was well regarding gravity. For some reason, he imagined that he would enter the airport to the sounds of the Chili Peppers. *Now that is a lie.* But it was just silence, cool air, an escalator down to customs. He assumed that was the right direction. What? They could just send him backward to where he belonged. But he was dead on, engaged in a snaking line, waiting to have his passport stamped with the logo of approval. *Stamp.* He moved on, headed out of the airport, then back inside. Along the way, he spotted an ATM and withdrew 400 soles, good for tips and purchases in the jungle from the inevitable craftspeople. To reach domestic departures, he had to exit the airport into the cool (67 degrees) air of Lima and confront a slew of taxi drivers, all beckoning him with encouraging words. Following the signs for the departure gates, he stumbled into a vast food court packed with hungry souls eating McDonald's and China Wok. A chicken place seemed authentic, but he chose China Wok, hoping for some sweet-and-spicy chicken, maybe some General Tso's. He ordered the Mandarin chicken, but they were fresh out, and he settled for what the young lady called "salt chicken." It looked sweet and sour to him. The meal came with a drink in a tiny cup, but there was no ice, which was interesting. It reminded him of the warm sodas he drank in Nigeria all those years ago. Maybe he would write a novel(s) about that. There were no tables, and he wandered, soon latching onto a couple who seemed to be in the dying throes of their meal.

Lucky, and he snagged their table and soon learned that his "salty chicken," even though it looked like sweet and sour chicken, was indeed just moist and salty. Oh well.

He decided to find a bar where he could sit, write, and drink, and he found it at Tanta, a large, square restaurant with empty chairs at high tables and a well-stocked bar. A woman sat across and to his left, with two empty chairs off to his right, which soon filled. The waiter was fast and presented Daniel with an English menu. Daniel perused the drinks and settled on a Peruvian craft beer, Ragnarovich, eight percent alcohol. The bottle looked old school, a very light amber, making the liquid look silver until you poured.

He drank and wrote, moving from eight pages to sixteen within an hour. The protagonist was nearing Lima and would soon eat at China Wok, then settle in for Peruvian craft beer at a place called Tanta. Two young girls, perhaps fifteen, sat across from him, and they reminded Daniel so much of Chelsea and Samantha. After three beers and up to twenty pages, he ordered a double shot of Jack Daniels on the rocks, determined to make the most of the evening. People came and went. He wrote. A pressure building in his bladder. The sound system sending out the mellifluous and dulcet tones of Freddie Mercury. And so the clock struck midnight.

Day Two

The Jack worked on him, and it was nearly two a.m.,

the place still hopping. He drew his writing to a close, paid his bill, and made his way to gate 19. The flight to Iquitos would leave at five-fifteen. He had enjoyed his whiskey buzz, but now felt an urge to eat. At a Dunkin' Donuts, he ordered a single chocolate donut, glissando, and a cup of coffee. He took his time, wandering until he reached the gate. He sat and decided to rest his eyes, but soon found his head snapping as sleep wanted to take over.

Finally, he was in his seat on Latin American Airlines, sitting near the front beside a window. The plane was packed and serviced by a jolly trim man who treated the passengers with a lighthearted touch. Soon, Daniel was asleep, having tried to read, and he awoke to a dimness, a redness in the sky beyond, the forest below blanketed with fog. There was a wide and winding river, but he wasn't sure if it was the Amazon. It didn't seem big enough and was perhaps the Itaya or Nanay. Iquitos, he'd read, was the world's largest city (nearly half a million souls) not accessible by road, but only by air or river.

All was green and lush as the plane landed, the morning still dull. He walked the hundred feet or so from the plane to the terminal. Inside were many people, waiting with signs. Someone from the tour he signed up for was supposed to meet him and take him to his hotel. But he did not see his name. Outside was an even bigger crowd—family and friends of those on board. A group of twenty men all locked eyes with Daniel, some saying Taxi and others saying Moto.

Daniel latched on quickly to an older man with a puckered tan face who drove a three-wheeled motorcycle, the moto. He told the man the name of his hotel, but wasn't sure the man understood. From prior experience, he knew that he could just be getting a ride to nowhere that he would be charged for.

The moto was loud and pressed forward, surrounded by other motos, motorcycles, cars, and trucks, all jostling for position, all spewing fumes. Daniel was surprised by the evident veneer of poverty, the shanties made of corrugated metal, the dirty streets, the many people walking. After ten minutes, the driver pulled over and stopped, but there was no hotel that Daniel could see. He just said No, No, and the old man careened back into traffic looking for the Amazon Apart Hotel. It took another five minutes, and Daniel saw a rough building that had an Amazon sign. It didn't look like the sleek building on the internet, and he was unsure if this was the right place. Reluctantly, he exited the moto and took a closer look, and there was a smaller sign: Amazon Apart. Si, si, he told the old man, and asked the price. Twenty soles. The smallest bill he had was a fifty, and the old man looked sad, searching his pockets. He only had a ten for change, which would mean that Daniel was giving a twenty-sole tip. Daniel resigned himself and paid, chalking it up to the subtle piracy of travel that one must endure on occasion.

Already, Daniel was feeling the stress of having to accommodate another language. Bits and pieces darted about in his brain. He'd lived for a month, a few years

back, in San Miguel de Allende, Mexico, and had taken
Spanish lessons there. Thinking in another language
was very stressful, especially if you were just on the edge
of getting it right. Walking to the registration desk, he
already knew he would sleep for a long time and that
he would hide, more or less, from his vulnerability. He
imagined the plight of refugees and their struggles with
language and culture, along with being unwanted. He
considered himself lucky, he supposed, to be able to
travel to another country knowing that he had a safe
return home in the works.

The receptionist did not speak English, but they
muddled through together, and Daniel took his key for
306, a real key attached to a piece of varnished wood
shaped something like a spade. The building inside was
made of cement blocks. The hallways were narrow, the
furniture made for people smaller than he was. Inside
his room, the TV was on, a fuzzy channel. The room
was warm, and he was warm in his jeans and short-
sleeve shirt, so he turned on the window AC, and it
worked.

Right away, his thoughts were of sleep, and he
undressed. The bed was king-size, with a two-inch foam
pad on top of the mattress. There was a sheet and a
lightweight brown blanket, which he crawled beneath
and closed his eyes. Voices and doors closing echoed
in the hallway, and soon he was asleep, waking around
five p.m. He hadn't had anything to drink since the
airport and felt it. He had not eaten since the donut as
well, but was not hungry at all. He found that when he

traveled, his need for food dropped nearly to zero. On the trip to San Miguel, he'd lost ten pounds, so much that he could just slip his jeans on without unbuttoning them. But he needed liquids.

In his room, needing water, he felt that hesitance that being in a strange place offers. There was a fear of facing the population, driven primarily by his lack of Spanish. He was an outsider and felt bad that he could afford to travel to Iquitos, while so many there could barely afford to survive, much less take a trip. And so, taking it slowly, he ventured to the hotel's restaurant. There were no other patrons. The music was loud. A woman came to him, said something, and then walked away. She was short, brown-skinned, and somewhat happy-faced. She had a little belly and wore tight polyester pants. He worried that he should wait for her to seat him. He watched from across the room as she performed unknown tasks. Had she forgotten him? He finally decided to sit down at a small table with two wine glasses. He crossed his legs and reminded himself to be patient. He was craving a cold drink, but she had not asked him if he wanted a drink, or had she?

Finally, she came with a menu. He couldn't remember the word for drink and let the moment pass. He perused the menu in Spanish, and there were several fish dishes. He wanted to try the various fish that came from the nearby mighty rivers, but settled on something familiar, a pollo con arroz dish that he knew he could handle. The price was 25 soles, about 8 dollars. And then, to his surprise, the waitress brought him a small pitcher of a lightly yellow drink and a glass. He had no idea what it was and asked. She told him, and he immediately forgot the name. The drink was sweet and refreshing, like cotton candy and pineapple mixed. By the time his plate arrived, he had drunk three-fourths.

The plate was huge, piled with rice, two fried chicken cutlets, a fried egg, and a salad that contained thin ribbons of what tasted like lemongrass. He wasn't hungry in the least and struggled to eat one piece of chicken and a third of the rice. He took his time, hoping that his stomach would accept more. He finished off his drink and motioned the waitress over. He felt bad about leaving so much food. Delicioso, he said, hoping she would understand. She reminded him that the price was 25 soles, as if he might request a discount. He just said Gracias and paid with a 100-sole bill. She had to leave to get change, and as soon as she was back, she sat behind the counter and began to devour his leftovers without shame. Daniel approached, glancing into a cooler with soft drinks. He purchased a Coke and an Inka Kola, a bright yellow drink.

Dark by now, he returned to his room, passing by a tiny pool where splashed a couple of kids. The first thing he did was drink the Coke and take his meds. He had decided to continue his meds at half-strength before any ayahuasca that he might encounter and let the cards fall as they may. That would be the next day, if the jungle tour he had booked actually came through. He worried that it was a scam since they had failed to pick him up from the airport, and began to wonder if he should contact the original retreat, Pitarika, that he had booked, to see if they would let him back in. That seemed like a sure bet. The lady there, Monika, always returned his emails, and he felt hopeful and sent her the email. The internet in his room was painfully slow, but it worked.

He was still sleepy, but decided to watch TV for a while. There were ninety or so channels, and he started with number eleven. Everything was in Spanish. He landed on a hardcore porn site called Venus. Two women were naked and making out. One woman had a terrible boob job. He could see the silicone implants outlined clearly beneath her two pierced nipples. He kept flipping and soon wound up on a show that minimized his need to understand the words, a guy building a custom roadster out of an old VW Beetle body.

Day Three

The next morning, he awoke around eight. He had read that there was a breakfast buffet, but still wasn't hungry, but was very thirsty. He stood and downed some Inka Kola, deciding just to go back to bed. He was partly hesitant because he would have to explore the hotel to find the buffet, and then perhaps find out that there was no buffet. So, back to bed he went, soon dreaming strange dreams.

He woke around noon and checked his email. Monika from Pitarika had replied, saying that she would put him back on the list. He was overjoyed and ceased to worry about possibly being ripped off by the other jungle-trip outfit. Pitarika was the real thing and legitimate. He looked forward to meeting Don Pedro, the shaman at Pitarika. Before his family had convinced him not to go to Pitarika, there had been much talk of everyone wanting a photo of Daniel and Don Pedro. It was Daniel, coming off his meds, who had gotten everyone alarmed while at the beach. He now seemed to be taking the long way around a short horse to arrive at his original goal. He decided that he would not tell them of his change in plans until he returned home safe and sound.

Daniel slept the sleep of the dead, waking around five p.m. No hunger, just a tremendous thirst. He looked in the mirror and saw a crazy man, eyelids sagging, hair askew. He needed at least thirty minutes to wake up to look and feel normal. He planned to exit the hotel and head left until he found a tienda that sold drinks. The sky was cloudy and gray, the air warm. He had expected that he would break out in deep sweats due to the humidity, but strolling, he only felt the rise of a slight moisture on his back. Surprisingly, most of the businesses on the dirty street were closed, the street with moderate traffic, almost exclusively with motos and motorcycles.

The small shops were tightly packed. A beefy woman was sweeping trash down the sidewalk and gutter. He passed a tiny hair salon, a man sitting there waiting for customers. For three blocks he walked, feeling that he was on a movie set and that he was really in California. He passed two restaurants, hesitating at each, but soon reached a tiny store that sold what he needed. The man inside was short with a barrel chest and a mustache. Arrayed in tiny piles were cookies, crackers, and chips. Daniel requested a bottle of water, agua, largo. What he needed to say was grande. And so a little game went back and forth as he tried to get the sizes of drinks he wanted. It took a minute, and a few laughs, but soon he had a large water, a regular Coke, and Inka Cola with packets of Oreos.

Feeling triumphant, he turned back, carrying his precious liquids. A man had joined the woman who was sweeping. She had made quite a pile of cardboard and dirt. On the sidewalk, a small drinking party had emerged with beer and music. He walked around them, wishing to join them. At some point, he worried he had passed the hotel and began scrutinizing the signs as he went by. He was relieved to see the sign, Amazon Apart, and soon arrived at his room. Daniel first undressed, having begun to sweat, and then took large swallows of the water and opened the Coke. His anxiety seemed to lower now that he had accomplished his task. He would not die from dehydration, and he would have the experience of the original retreat as he had planned. It was fate, right?

Day Four

Such a long night of tossing and turning, worrying that he couldn't find the meeting place, worried that he would be late for the bus, worried about letting his family know that he was really going. Out on the street, Daniel picked the shadiest character, the most ruthless moto driver. He could see the sneer, the challenge of charging the gringo four times the going rate. He figured he'd be lucky to get away with 50 soles, about 12 dollars. And so he bumped along in thin morning traffic, each pothole racing to his spine. He could tell the driver was confused and showed him the name of the hotel again on his cell phone. And there he was, a tourist with his backpack and no doubt his pockets jingling with gold. The meeting place was the Yellow Hotel, and a young woman walked his way. She was with Pitarika and introduced herself as Simone. She was short, with ringlets of black hair, and spoke with a soft French accent. A couple of others were already there, and Daniel introduced himself.

Right away, a hardened character with two plastic shopping bags approached Daniel. This man knew about the meeting place for the retreat and brought special items the attendees would need and had perhaps forgotten, such as flashlights and ponchos. Daniel said, Gracias, and indicated no, but the man persisted, but not too aggressively, and that won Daniel over. He inquired about the price of a flashlight. Twenty soles. Overpriced, but what the hell? The man seemed truly touched once Daniel acquiesced. Cuanto cuesta? Daniel asked again, and the price had not budged. And in this manner, through three other salespeople, Daniel acquired a flashlight, four ayahuasca necklaces, a packet of jungle tobacco cigarettes known as mapacho, an elaborate pipe, and a handcrafted fan.

Over the next hour, the group grew, assembling itself for adventure. There were Lisa and Janice from Arizona, who lived together, but were not lesbians. There was Doug from Arkansas, dark, angular, and swarthy, who talked a mile a minute. Manuel, quiet and tattooed. Dan, an older gentleman with a smoker's voice from Canada. Others hailed from New Zealand, Romania, Cincinnati, Stamford, and Los Angeles. Also helping out with Simone were two Peruvians, Carlos and Ramon, who spoke limited English.

To begin their journey into the jungle, the group boarded a small bus with small seats, whizzing deep into slums, past buildings of corrugated metal with dirt floors, chickens wandering in and out. The sky was high, light blue, and covered with scattered clouds. Not hot enough to sweat from walking or sitting. The bus, within twenty minutes, soon came to a small, snaking river, the Rio Nanay. Down a slick embankment of packed sandy soil, Daniel stepped carefully. A long, colorful wooden boat covered with a palm-leaf roof waited. The helpers loaded the bags first, then the group boarded, taking care to keep the boat balanced. Powered by a Honda motor with an extended propeller shaft, the boat eased into the open water, soon reaching the main channel.

Scruffy banks led upward to greenery and open fields. The boat tooled along, not in a hurry. Up on a slope, preceded by a muddy flat, lay the small town of

Manacamiri, an outpost of Iquitos. Sleepy, inhabitants walked the long sidewalk that ran its length past corrugated tin houses with palm frond roofs. Walking more or less in silence, Daniel stopped to buy a bottle of fruit juice for fifty cents, which he drained. He was supposed to have been following an ayahuasca diet two weeks prior, but had not felt like doing without salt, sugar, oil, and spices.

Beneath a hot, distant sun, the sidewalk gave way to a dirt path and soon bore right onto a wider path, rutted, grassy, muddy. Off to the sides were cleared fields and the occasional house. The retreat center's leader, Don Pedro, owned forty hectares of land in the area, many cultivated with fruit trees such as banana and apple, and also coffee and cacao. There was not much to see on the forty-five-minute walk to Pitarika, and a crude sign welcomed them. Don Pedro was there to meet them, wearing an orange Stihl t-shirt and shorts. He just looked like a normal guy—short with a belly and a broad smile, good teeth. The path led to the main camp area, which housed the maloka—the large, round hut with a steeply thatched roof where the ayahuasca ceremonies would take place—then a screened dining hut, a bathroom/shower, a dining hall for workers, and a cooking hut. The group milled about, chatting excitedly. The biggest talker of all, Doug, never rested, engaging everyone with how cool the experience was so far, how mind-blowing the ceremonies would be. Doug was thirty-five, with slicked-back black hair and an angular face with deep glancing eyes.

In the maloka, three staff members, led by Simone, oriented the group to the camp and explained what would happen over the following week. Simone was French and studying the medicinal plants of the forest. Carlos, a helper, was tall and beefy with a square face and spoke the least English. Ramon, another helper, was lithe and skinny with a slight lisp, short, but with reasonably good English. All were dressed casually, much like the shorts and sandals of the visitors.

Daniel took stock of the group, and it seemed a good one. There was a bit of wearing the heart on the sleeve. Everything was Amazing! The two women of Daniel's age, who turned out not to be lesbians, lived together in New Mexico. Janice looked after Lisa. Lisa was nonstop positive but had several health issues, including a bad gut and poor vision, of which she hoped to be cured. Janice looked to be the free-loving hippy who would give her last penny to a beggar. She, too, was enthusiastic, as if over-the-top jubilance was necessary for the ayahuasca to work.

Others in the group included Randy, from Cleveland, with a soul patch and a gift for gab, knowing the latest cool bands and sources of vegan foods. He put bee pollen on his salad. Manuel from Los Angeles kept to himself, very quiet but not shy. Like Doug, he was heavily tattooed, as was the New Zealander, Lemmy. Daniel had tattoos on his upper arms, and it looked as if everyone had at least one tattoo, except for Lisa. You don't put a bumper sticker on a Bentley, and Lisa had laughed. Vlad was Russian, tattooed all over, but living in Connecticut. Like James, he was a carpenter. James from Limerick, Ireland, was thin, shy, and hard to understand. Sandra from Minnesota, a blonde with a big smile, and a married couple, Jose and Sabina, from Los Angeles. The man with the cigarette voice was named Dan, a Canadian and practitioner of chakras and I energy. Finally, Elena was from Romania, living in Stockholm, and attending school there. She was tall, very, very thin, blonde, and prone to blush and smile. Very pretty, but she seemed to be an acquaintance of Vlad.

Next, Simone led the group around the small lake on a boardwalk. As they approached a tambo, she assigned each one. Daniel received numero seis and set off uphill to settle in. The tambo was a square hut with a thatched roof. The entire structure was screened, but there were no mosquitoes. The dry and rotted wall boards only came up to his waist, and then it was screen. He plopped his heavy backpack on the simple wooden bed with a thin foam mattress. Behind a divider sat a raw toilet without a seat. There was a bucket of water to flush with. Nicely settled among the trees, the tambo was neither cool nor hot. Time seemed to have stopped, and so Daniel moved his pack and lay on the bed. Sounds of the jungle, a soft insect noise punctuated with pops and coos, birds he imagined.

Not meaning to, Daniel slept through lunch. He checked his phone, which amazingly had one bar of service. Groggy, he pulled on his rain boots, bought specially for the trip. At the camp center, beside the dining hut, he found a small group gathered, talking. Doug was the center of attention, ranting about how trees communicate with one another and about how fucking amazing trees and mushrooms were. The others were nodding their full appreciation. Daniel spied a white cat with blue eyes and navigated that way. He missed his cats, and this cat reminded him of a cat he had lost a year earlier. This cat was a he with huge balls, and lay on the bench like a little lion. Daniel stroked his back. The cat arched and stretched in appreciation. For a couple of minutes, he was lost in the world of this cat.

He was on the edge of the group, listening to the banter. Essentially, he was shy and quiet when around a group. He did best when the group was small, perhaps two or three. He decided to explore the dining hut and found platters of bananas, apples, and grapes. There was filtered water, and he filled his Nalgene bottle. He took a handful of grapes and went outside. He popped one in, and it had a very thick skin and was slimy like a mus-cadine. He swallowed and put the grapes in his pocket.

At 3:30 was the first group circle, where everyone would get to know one another and be diagnosed by Don Pedro. Daniel dreaded sitting on the floor of the maloka on a thin pad. Most of the group could sit with legs crossed, but his ligaments and tendons said, No. First to speak was Sandra, and she referred to ayahuasca as Mother Ayahuasca. Sandra was there for healing, es-pecially regarding her relationship with her son and the absent father. The subject pained her greatly, and she wept. Simone interpreted for Don Pedro, who nodded his head, said some wise words, and then told Simone what plant medicines Sandra needed.

Around the circle they went, and apparently everyone was there for some sort of spiritual therapy, which caught Daniel off guard. He was there just to experience the mysterious ayahuasca, letting it take him wherever it may. When it came his turn to speak, he said that he wished to see inside, that there was something that he needed to see. The group murmured their appreciation. He received his prescription, five plant abstracts written on a small piece of paper. The circle lasted for over an hour, and Daniel was about to go crazy sitting on the pad, changing his position every twenty seconds to keep from falling asleep and to relieve the pain in his limbs and back. The creeping sensation of religion crossed his mind.

Everyone took their slips of paper to the pharmacy, where a short woman named Ruby took their prescriptions and poured up special green cocktails for each. Daniel sat in the plastic chair and took his cup, which looked like pesto. He threw it back and swallowed, and it was like mowed grass. He drank some water to wash away the vegetal taste. He was to take the medicine at eight in the morning and five in the evening. Ugh.

Dinner was at six, and he made it half an hour late. He only wanted to sleep. He looked at his plate. There was a dry salad with coarse green leaves. There was a piece of fish baked in a tomato sauce. There was a perfect mound of rice and a perfect mound of lentils. He took a bite. No salt. No spices. His throat rebelled, and he swallowed hard, washing the bites down with warm water. The fish was tender and was the most satisfying thing on his plate, but the lack of salt seemed wrong, and each bite was a chore, although conversation around the table was pleasant. For dessert, there was fruit and hot tea, no sugar.

With his headlamp, Daniel walked back to his tambo, the darkness taking him. At first, he was lost, but then recognized the two tambos to his left and then took a right uphill. The forest sounds had intensified, a dull chorus of crickets backing frogs and tropical birds. He had brought the book he needed to read, but it was disjointed and poorly written. He had his cheap laptop to get some writing in. He planned to write about his experience with ayahuasca using a narrator who tells the story of a young man similar to himself. He just decided he was tired and lay down, soon taken in by the night sounds and the exhaustion of seeing new things. He slept.

Day Five

They were to rise at six and meet in the maloka, where they would be administered a plant product called piñon colorado. This would be followed by three liters of water slaked as fast as possible to induce vomiting. Daniel received his dose and swallowed, again, a powerful grass taste. He lit into the water, the first liter, and drank. Carlos and Ramon raced around refilling glasses. Daniel drank another, feeling fat with water.

He forced down another liter, water spreading into his beard. Already sounds of vomiting, and it came like a subway down the tube. He vomited deep and steady into an orange bucket, over and over, until he sat exhausted, his face glistening with water. He was done.

The thought of a saltless breakfast made Daniel queasy, so he skipped. The first ceremony was that night, and there was a convocation after breakfast in the maloka, where the ceremony would be described in detail. Simone led the session, and everyone listened intently as it was their first time, except for Jose, who had done ayahuasca four times before, all with Don Pedro. He was quite the disciple of Don Pedro and described him as a mountain of a man. As Daniel had already read, Simone informed them that there would be vomiting after ingesting the ayahuasca and perhaps also diarrhea. Great news. Helpers would be available to walk them to the bathroom if needed. One only needed to knock on the floor three times if assistance was required. Daniel imagined a night of fireworks, perhaps a darkness like that of the end of times.

He skipped lunch but made himself go to dinner. The saltless beans, salad, and a chicken dish with beets made him just a little sick. He quickly washed away the blandness with plain water, feeling very full, having eaten very little. The ceremony began at seven, so he hurried back to his tambo for a rest. It was going to happen. He had gone to a lot of trouble to be there, and expectations were high.

Daniel aappeared at the maloka to discover that he

was the last one to arrive. In the dark, he searched for
an empty mat and wound up between Elena and James.
The foam pad was thin, a single candle burning in the
middle of the round room. Within a few minutes, Don
Pedro entered, dressed in white and barefoot. A woman
with a small pitcher of ayahuasca accompanied him.
All was quiet and Carlos tapped a brass cymbal, letting
the note linger and eke like smoke. This was followed
by a few lulling bars on the harmonica, sad and calling. Daniel shifted on the mat, trying to focus on this
Mother Ayahuasca.

There was a brief session of haunting pan flute, the
darkness magnifying the music. And then it began,
the call to receive the infamous jungle drug, ayahuasca. Carlos snuffed the candle, sending the room into
complete darkness, moonlight hesitating until eyes
adjusted. Don Pedro sat in his chair, flanked by the
older woman holding the brew and Simone on the
other side. First, Carlos made the rounds, dripping a
perfumed water into waiting hands, which was then
bathed onto the face and arms. Then, the first person to
Don Pedro's left was called, and Daniel could not see
what was happening. One by one, each went forward
and returned to their mats. Soon it was Elena's turn,
and then Daniel. He stood and approached Don Pedro
in his chair, silent. Daniel could not sit cross-legged, so
kneeled instead and even found that somewhat painful.
You are ready to take the medicine? said Simone. Daniel whispered, Yes. He watched as Don Pedro held a tall
shot glass illuminated by a small flashlight. His assis-

tant poured very carefully from the small pitcher. Don
Pedro picked up a cigarette from between his feet, the
mapacho jungle tobacco, and blew smoke three times
into the glass, then held it forth for Daniel. Daniel nodded, received the glass, and tossed it back like a Jaeger
bomb. The taste was sickening, a mix of sour wine, soy
sauce, tree bark, and chewing tobacco. Daniel stood
and returned to his mat, wishing away the foul taste.

On his back, Daniel waited for screams of delight,
slurs of terror, evidence of hallucinations. But it was
only silence as the others received their medicine. Daniel monitored himself, imagining that at any moment
he would fly into another dimension, but nothing
seemed to be happening.

The last of the group received their doses, and all
was quiet. Without ceremony, Don Pedro launched
into an icaro, a song to help one along the journey to
health and healing through the sacred vine. Rhythmic
and primal, his voice, almost chanting, was accompanied by palm frond shakers. The song was quite long,
and Don Pedro picked up the next song soon after
finishing the first. Daniel was still swallowing, trying
to get the taste of the ayahuasca from his mouth. All
was quiet around the room. No one was up dancing or
talking in gibberish. There was no bedlam or mayhem,
no mass loss of control. But the vomiting did begin,
halfway through the second icaro.

Daniel knew that it would take at least thirty
minutes for something to happen and figured that he
at least should be feeling queer, but felt terribly normal.

He wished for a sign that his body was in the throes of a new experience, but he did not even feel nauseous. He looked to either side, and Elena and James appeared to be on planet Earth, much as he was. Was this it? Would the next four and a half hours just be Don Pedro singing? Already, it was somewhat of a torture to just lie on the floor on the puny mat, and he shifted to his side.

And Don Pedro continued with the icaros, earnest and mesmerizing. As the hour passed, there was guitar, played by someone unknown. There was more vomiting, a few going to the toilets. On his back, Daniel did feel a peace deep within, but had no visions, no shooting colors, no angels or demons. He wondered if he'd been ripped off. What had he drunk? Just some jungle juice, boiled cigar butts maybe?

After two hours, there was a break in the singing, and someone was coming around. It was a young man with a soft face, and he asked if Daniel wanted more. Oh, so perhaps it would take a second dose to get some effect? Daniel indicated yes, and soon it was his turn again. He stood, stretched, and wobbled. Things were off balance. He went before Don Pedro, kneeling. As before, Simone was there. She asked him if he'd had any visions, and he had not. She seemed surprised and asked him if he wanted another dose, and he said, Yes. Don Pedro held the glass, and the old woman poured. Dreading the taste, Daniel took the glass and threw the grainy liquid to the back of his throat. Oh God, it was awful, and he belched, staggering back to his place on the floor.

Daniel really felt now that the love and rockets would appear. Another hour dragged by, going from side to side on his mat. He had to go to the bathroom and stood. Carlos came for him and took his arm, leading him out of the maloka and to the bathroom. It was diarrhea, but he'd already had a touch that day. Back inside, Don Pedro was making his way around the room, singing personal icaros to each person, blessing them, blowing smoke into their faces and into their hands folded in prayer. More guitar, more singing, just more peace, but no psychedelic show. Daniel, at some point, just gave up and relegated himself to a fate of just inner peace, but it was an inner peace that he sometimes felt with his antidepressant. At midnight, the roosters all crowed as if to announce the end of the ceremony, and twenty minutes later, it was finished. One by one, people stood and, with flashlights, stumbled to their tambos. Daniel found walking awkward and had trouble making a straight line, but he did not feel drunk or high. For five hours, he'd lain on the floor of the maloka, being subjected to a one-man concert. He'd not had anything close to a psychedelic experience and remembered that marijuana did not affect him either. Perhaps he was immune, but most likely it was his antipsychotic medication.

Back at the tambo, it was quite dark. He drank water, decided he would take his meds, and considered doing some work, perhaps reading, but it was not in the cards, and he just lay down, slowly drifting into sleep, the forest nightlife singing its own songs.

Day Six

He awoke the next morning, just in time for breakfast at seven, but the thought of a saltless meal made him sick. He went to the dining hut anyway for an apple. Lisa was just coming down from the pharmacy and told him not to forget his medicine. Daniel murmured but was caught and ascended the dirt stairway to receive the green elixir. God, it was bad, and he hurried to the fruit tray in the dining hut to wash away the harsh chlorophyll taste. Others were there eating breakfast, preparing for the group circle at nine, declaiming that the experience the previous night had been awesome, the visions mind-blowing. The general hyperbole extended to one another, Doug praising Jose as godlike. Jose responded with how amazing Doug was, and so on.

Always needing a nap, Daniel walked back to his tambo for an hour-long siesta and woke to his cell phone alarm as if seconds had passed. He arrived at the group circle, being next to the last to arrive, and took his place on the floor. Don Pedro was there to respond to their testimonies, translated by Simone. Right away, Daniel knew he was in trouble when James began a long soliloquy on his visions of strange creatures and bright colors. Daniel had not seen anything other than his mates on the floor, Don Pedro singing from his chair. But he'd had an epiphany of sorts. He'd not visited the graves of his grandparents, who had died more than ten years ago. It occurred to him that he still thought of them as being alive and had not accepted their deaths. So, that is what he shared with the group, announcing his plans to visit his grandparents' graves. It was the best he could do.

Group circle seemed to go on forever, and Daniel shifted and shuffled on his mat, arching his back, stretching his legs, leaning this way, leaning that way, desperate to sit in a chair or stand. Don Pedro's responses to the various testimonies spoke invariably of "the light within," of "balance," and of the fickle but demanding nature of Mother Ayahuasca. As soon as Don Pedro gave his response to Daniel, Daniel could not remember a word of what had been said, his eyes heavy, wishing only to sleep.

Finally, it was over, and Daniel walked as a zombie, feeling like an overstuffed mattress, back to his tambo, knowing that he would lapse into a deep sleep and miss lunch, which was fine. His rain boots scuffing the dry dirt, he could barely restrain himself from lying on the ground, perhaps gnawing on a root, and just dying, fading into nothing. He made it to his tambo and fell on his bed like a rock, cracking a board.

After taking his afternoon herbal concoction, Daniel self-administered a flower bath, which basically meant splashing water floating with flowers onto his skin and hair. It smelled good and was supposed to draw poisons from the body in preparation for Mother Ayahuasca. Doug was holding court with Randy in front of the dining hut, each affirming one another with mighty proclamations as others listened and nodded agreeably. Janice proclaimed that Sandra was a blessing. Sandra responded by acknowledging Janice's deep wisdom. Talk drifted to the second ceremony. Rumor was that the dose would be doubled upon request, and Daniel was hopeful for something more than just a deep peace and a drunken gait.

Daniel decided to give dinner a try, and one bite into the boiled chicken with yellow beets, he knew he'd made a mistake. He needed salt badly, plus he disliked the earthy taste of beets. One spoon at a time, he tackled the flavorless rice and beans, washing it down with lukewarm water. He felt more nauseated eating than he did consuming the ayahuasca. After eating and exchanging pleasantries, there was an hour or so until the ceremony, and he sauntered back to his hut, thinking of his daughters, thinking of how lucky he was, thinking fondly of his mountain bike. His stomach gurgled, and he hurried to the tambo.

He poured water into the toilet from the white bucket and discovered that he had a light bulb on the wall with an outlet. He'd heard there was power for a few hours each day, but had totally missed the light. His phone had died, so he plugged it in with a voltage reducer and hoped he could just lie on his bed for a while without falling asleep and missing the ceremony.

At ten till seven, he walked back to the maloka, and he was the last to arrive. In the darkness, he searched for an empty mat, feeling his way like a blind man. Don Pedro had not yet arrived, so that was good. As soon as Daniel sat down and leaned forward on his arms, Carlos came to the center of the room and lit the candle. This was followed by the gentle scraping of a cymbal and then simple notes on a harmonica. Daniel realized that he was in for a five-hour ordeal, squirming on a thin pad, and hoped that the double dose would work its magic on him. He'd also resumed full dosing of his meds and was feeling somewhat more normal, and hoped perhaps that the meds would boost the power of the ayahuasca. Or did the meds block the effects? He wasn't sure, but from the first night's mild experience, he felt that he had room to play with fire.

Don Pedro entered, accompanied by his assistant, the older woman who carried the pitcher of ayahuasca. Carlos doused the candle, and the second ceremony was underway as he went around with the perfumed water, which was rather strong but pleasant. Daniel massaged it into his hair and face, seeming to be on the edge of a high dive. Would there be water in the pool?

He had wound up on the far side of the room and so was third to last to receive Mother Ayahuasca. All was quiet against the backdrop of crickets, frogs, and birds night calling. A brilliant moon was out, sending in a glaze of light that only deepened the shadows. He approached the shaman and went to his knees. Simone asked him if he would like the double dose, and he said, "Yes." After blowing smoke over the tall shot glass of brown liquid, Don Pedro held the glass out to Daniel. Dreading the taste, he knocked it back and shuddered. He had trouble standing and returned to his mat to await his fate, gentle sounds of puking and gagging coming from around the room.

And then Don Pedro entered into his long night of singing the icaros to guide them along the path of receiving visions. Daniel felt that he had always known the songs and could feel the rhythms imprinting his brain. He guessed that half an hour had passed, and he had felt nothing other than being terribly relaxed, which he considered to be of some significance. How was it that he was shifting from hip to hip and not completely miserable as the time slipped by, song after song? He wasn't nauseated, had no diarrhea, didn't need to pee—which was a miracle—and had no visions. He tried closing his eyes and summoning the hallucinations, but nothing would come, just the relentless songs pounding into him an extreme peace. He thought of home, Samantha and Chelsea, Remy, his cats, his dog, apple pie.

Two hours passed, but it seemed like maybe one, and Daniel found himself receiving a second double dose. Simone was surprised that he had not had any visions. He wondered if he was somehow immune to mind-altering natural drugs. He lay back down and tried again to summon a vision, something that spoke of an altered state. He was at peace but mildly desperate for results, but to no avail.

When the roosters crowed, Daniel knew that it was midnight, and the ceremony was over within ten min-utes. Like zombies, bodies rose from around the room, lit now by a candle, glowing in the dark. A few stayed put, but most were headed back to their tambos. Hun-gry for an apple, Daniel stood and walked jaggedly, off balance. He turned on his headlamp and, with passing nods, made his way to the dining hut where others had the same idea. He just took an apple and, with his rain boots scuffing the earth, he ate and walked, weaving back and forth, wondering what it all meant.

Back in his tambo, his phone was charged, and he checked his email, watching as dozens of new messages appeared. Even though he'd just been supine for five hours, he was drawn to the bed, where he decided to read for a while. His mind felt clear, not drugged at all. The book, though, was still dry and not well written. He put the book aside, slept, and dreamed vivid dreams.

Day Seven

Daniel slept in late, his hips sore from lying on the mat and the thin mattress on his bed. There was just enough water to swallow his meds and brush his teeth. He felt a bit groggy, but not hungover from what had been a hefty dose of ayahuasca. He was hungry, but had missed breakfast, and group circle was in half an hour. He was supposed to have gone for his traditional medicine, but had more or less written that off. The taste was just foul and didn't seem to affect his ability to experience the ayahuasca. He sauntered into the main camp area, and Doug was there holding court, gesticulating, punching the air with his fist, and proclaiming the beauty of the forest and the wisdom of Don Pedro. Daniel just grunted and went into the dining hut for an apple. The

Cocamas, an indigenous people living nearby, were supposed to visit.

Back outside, sitting on a bench, Daniel engaged in small talk with Lisa. She seemed to have had an improvement in her vision, which had been compromised by steroids years ago. Simone was squeezing milky drops from the stem of a local grass. And then it was time for the group circle, where everyone shared their previous night's experience and received feedback from Don Pedro. Daniel lit a mapacho cigarette and took his place on the floor of the maloka, dreading the awkward sitting position.

Daniel listened as Jose spoke of his amazing visions. He had seen strange creatures who read recipes to him from a large book. Don Pedro took all of this in and responded about the light and the love that are inside us all, and that we must seek the wisdom of others to live a life of reflection. Daniel wracked his brain for something to say, and the only thing he could come up with was that he had not vomited, had not any visions, but had experienced an extreme peace. Don Pedro, in his reserved manner, speaking with his hands, spoke for a minute, and Simone translated. Daniel listened, but as before, could not remember a word of what was said, being so uncomfortable, wishing for something sweet to drink and something salty to eat. He supposed he was somehow not in the right spirit and had basically decided not to do a third ceremony, but did not share that with the group.

After the agony of group circle, which made him

feel slightly comatose, Simone announced that the Co-camas were there and to gather on the benches near the large pond. It was very hot and Daniel was sweating as soon as he sat down. Everyone was genuinely interested in the dance that the tribespeople would be performing. They must have been hiding in the woods, and they burst into song and drums, streaming into the circular dirt area, each one unloading arts and crafts on a set of empty benches across from the group. They did this in quite a hurry, then re-gathered, breaking out into song once again, accompanied by drums. There were a dozen women and two teenage boys, all dressed in white with jet-black hair and deep brown skin.

One dance led to another, and then, surprise, Simone shouted for the group to join the dancers. Daniel soon found himself in a whirling circle, going round and round, trying not to fall. He was holding hands with a young girl, and she whipped him around at such a pace that he felt he would fall. The dance dissolved, and a circle formed. A wooden staff representing an anaconda was produced, and a dancer in the middle twirled and then passed the staff to Janice, who was soon in the center doing her own dance as everyone clapped. Soon it was Daniel's turn, and he twirled the brightly colored staff like a baton and did his best to make his feet move to some sort of rhythm. He felt a thrill and then passed the snake to the first set of hands, Sandra, who continued the dance.

And then, just like that, the dancing and drums finished, and the women and girls rushed to their stations, ready to sell their wares. Daniel had his wallet and saw that it would soon be empty, but why not? He inspected bracelets, hand-woven bags, and paintings. When he was finished, he had spent nearly 300 soles on several objects, including a black mask carving, all gifts for his daughters. Sweating profusely, he gathered his items and, nodding to everyone, made his way back to the tambo for a little siesta before lunch, wondering how he would break the news to Simone and Carlos that he would not be taking part in the ceremony that night.

The heat lulled him into a drowse, and he woke in time for lunch, which was more fish and fried plantains. Chatter in the dining hut was lively, and he made his way through the bland food one slow bite at a time. After lunch was painting with natural colors, such as turmeric and purple corn. A woman named Lenora would interpret the paintings in the maloka. Daniel was at a table with Manuel, Randy, and Lisa. He tried not to look at their paintings and focused on his rectangle of cloth. He decided that his work needed a center and a perspective, so made some hash marks and lines. He then decided that he would just dash short lines and curls, dipping into the six paints at random. He took his time but was finished within twenty minutes, satisfied with his work. He noticed that Randy and Lisa had both drawn peace signs. Manuel had drawn flowers and a sun.

A few of the group gathered in front of the dining hut, just talking of this and that. Doug was expounding on the wisdom of Don Pedro, stating that PhDs came to study his work. It soon became apparent that Lenora was taking at least half an hour for each painting, and Daniel didn't feel like waiting hours, so he returned to his tambo with the one thing that was always on his mind: sleep. He set his alarm for four and crawled onto the bed, sweating, and soon lapsed into a deep sleep, dreaming and dreaming of what he did not know upon waking. But he had an epiphany of sorts. He decided that he had not been ready for the first two ceremonies, that he had not surrendered completely to Mother Ayahuasca, and that somehow he was now ready. A little thrill shot through him, and he was on for the ceremony that night with renewed vigor. He felt excited, and upon joining the group in front of the dining hut, he made his revelation, drawing many nods of appreciation.

With his newfound purpose, Daniel drifted toward the large pond, or was it a small lake? The water was dark brown as if dyed by tree bark and was surrounded by towering palms. He approached a small floating dock and saw Simone swimming on the far side, coming back, and decided that there must not be any piranhas. Why not take a dip? Simone swam to the dock and emerged from the water. For a brief instance, she smiled, and with water streaming down her face and body, she looked stunning. Her right nipple was exposed, and Daniel tried to just look at her face. Then, without further ado, Daniel removed his shirt and dove into the water in his biking pants, feeling the warm top layer swirl with cooler layers beneath. And then Dan jumped in, doing a cannonball, followed by Janice and James.

Daniel treaded water, waiting to see if fish nibbled at his legs as they did in the lakes back home. The water was refreshing, and he felt reborn, floating on his back and staring at the big circle of cloudy sky. He felt light, buoyant. He imagined riding his mountain bike up the big hill back home, imagined seeing his daughters, imagined pecan pie. He floated for about ten minutes and then pulled himself onto the dock, thoroughly refreshed. He had not had a shower since arriving. He then took his flower bath, with little bits of green and flower petals sticking to his body. He'd decided to pass on dinner, hoping that would help enhance his experience that night at seven.

Back in his tambo, he changed into dry clothes. He noted that there were no mosquitoes and that he had not needed to bring his little container of DEET, and wondered at that. He also had not seen giant bugs, which he had expected. The only wildlife, aside from the chickens, he had seen were small birds and one large turtle. There were small monkeys somewhere, but he did not see them. Once again, he set his alarm and reclined for a peaceful siesta, rising at six-thirty to make his way to the maloka, taking a few mapacho cigarettes with him. He'd brought cigars but thus far had not been tempted to smoke one.

He was the last to arrive at the maloka and stumbled around for the last empty mat. Doug called out to him, pointing the way, and Daniel took the spot

between him and Manuel. Daniel would be the second
to receive the ayahuasca. The routine was the same:
the candle, the cymbals, and the harmonica, followed
by the perfumed water that he rubbed in his hair. An
excitement had built within him, and he lay back with
his head on a pillow.

Don Pedro and his assistant entered, taking their
places. Simone joined them. Carlos doused the light,
washing the round room with the steep-pitched roof
in darkness. The rafters looked like bones or perhaps
a carousel. After Manuel, Daniel went forward, knelt,
and took a double dose. The taste right away sickened
him. He had brought a piece of gum and popped it in
after returning to his mat to begin the wait. It took half
an hour for everyone to receive their doses. And then
Don Pedro launched into his icaros, singing, chanting,
filling the maloka with his spirit.

Daniel relaxed and opened himself to the medicine, waiting for the visions to commence. After an
hour, nothing had happened, and he worried that he
was immune to the DMT in the ayahuasca brew. It was
the same with marijuana; nothing happened. The two
things he could count on to get him high were cigars
and alcohol. He redoubled his efforts to receive and
closed his eyes, concentrating. Briefly, there were bright
lights and a fleeting vision of a house on fire, the flames
leaping from the basement to the second and third
floors, but then it was gone. He despaired, knowing
that the night would be no different from the rest, and
began his ritual of turning from side to side, trying to

enjoy the peace the singing engendered.

When it came time for the second dose, he passed, as did a few others. All was quiet, except for Don Pedro's soothing, low-toned songs accompanied by his fistful of palm leaves that he shook vigorously. At one point, no longer able to lie down, Daniel stood, walked outside, and sat on the bench, gathering his thoughts. Manuel was there, but there was a rule of no talking. Daniel slipped into the dining hut, having forgotten his headlamp, and fumbled around until he found an apple. After the apple, he returned to his mat in the maloka, waiting for the roosters to crow to indicate that the ceremony would soon be over, and like clock-work, they chimed in at midnight as Don Pedro was making his rounds, singing over each body. And then it was over, the candle relit.

In silence, everyone stood and left. As usual, Daniel was off balance and staggered down the boarded path to his tambo, wide awake and intent on reading. The electricity was off, and he searched in the dark for his headlamp, soon finding it with the aid of a lighter. He took his book on reflective practice and began to read, smoking a cigar, but soon grew disinterested and retrieved the tiny laptop he had brought to write the story of a man named Daniel who went to the Amazon rainforest to an ayahuasca retreat. In the story, Daniel had decided to completely surrender to Mother Aya-huasca, but without result.

Day Eight

Daniel awoke, drank water, and used the toilet, pouring water from the bucket. He had been taking his meds, although there was supposed to be a danger of antidepressants interacting with ayahuasca, making it toxic. He wondered if his other two meds had somehow offset the ayahuasca. He took an antipsychotic, olanzapine. Maybe the antipsychotic was blocking the ayahuasca? He would really never know. He had not had any visions like his campmates.

He remembered that another tribe was scheduled to visit that morning, supposed to arrive at seven a.m. Daniel had spent all of his money on the last group. Around eight, he walked the two hundred feet or so into the camp. He saw Janice, and she told him that the breakfast had salt in it. That excited him, being hungry and thirsty. He peeked between the dining hut and the cooking hut and could see women from the tribe there, large, colorful paintings spread on the ground. But he had no more cash, so he decided to eat breakfast. He brought the fried plantain to his mouth and chewed. Salt! He moaned, and Dan, across from him, gave him a high-five. And the eggs with peppers! With salt!

Satisfied, Daniel drank a cup of hot chamomile tea, his ersatz coffee, which was not on the ayahuasca menu. As usual, he trotted back to his tambo, letting his eyes drowse in the rising heat. He kept his cell phone by his side, checking the time every few minutes, and then it was back for group circle. He had no idea what he would say. He had not had any visions or revelations, not even any good ideas. There was that intense and weird peaceful feeling, and he figured that he would just stick to that.

At nine, he returned to the maloka, and everyone was there. Today, Don Pedro was out, replaced by his understudy Omar, who also sang icaros and played the guitar. Restless, Daniel squirmed on his mat, trying to find a comfortable position. Most had taken the third ayahuasca dose, and Manuel was first to talk. He spoke of visions of his dead mother, whom he had not had a chance to say goodbye to. He spoke, almost out of breath, at the intensity of the vision. Everyone listened in silence. Omar chuckled and spoke at length, interpreted by Simone. Daniel could not hear the words, thinking only of returning home to see his daughters, to eat at McDonald's.

His turn came, and he admitted that he had not had any visions; he had only felt that sense of peace while listening to Don Pedro sing. Omar had little to say. Finally, the group circle was over, and Simone asked who would be taking the optional fourth dose. A few raised their hands. That night, instead of gathering in the maloka, Don Pedro would visit the tambos of those participating.

Exhausted, Daniel hung around for a few minutes speaking with Elena. He imagined she was twenty-five. She was tall, thin, blonde, and very attractive, and he felt shy around her. She seemed to be friends with Vlad, but he couldn't tell if they were a couple or not. He finished his mapacho cigarette and walked back to his tambo in slow motion. He checked his phone and had a text from his daughter. He was amazed to have cell phone service and replied, wondering what the cost would be. Onto the bed in a sweat he went and drowsed like an alligator, missing lunch.

He dragged himself from bed around four and decided to take a swim. He wore his biking shorts and hoped others would be in the water, but when he arrived, the pond was very still and quiet, a deep brown. He stood on the end of the floating dock and positioned himself. He realized he was still wearing his glasses and took them off. He sort of did a half flip into the water, feeling the cool mix with the warm. He still worried that there were piranhas and moved his legs and arms vigorously, as if that would protect him. He floated for a minute or two, and that was enough. He hauled himself out of the water, feeling cool and peaceful. He'd not been showering, and he felt somewhat clean from the dip.

Dinner that night had salt, and he devoured his chicken with boiled potatoes. He was missing having desserts and ate an apple. He hung around outside for a while, participating in the chatter mostly by listening. Those who were receiving the ceremony were heading back to their tambos, and so he did as well. The jungle sounds soothed him, crickets, frogs, and birds.

Back at his tambo, he decided to continue writing about the man at the ayahuasca retreat. The man had not had visions, was sleeping a lot, and would soon take a swim in the still pond. He had to use his headlamp as the keyboard on the cheap computer was not backlit.

The man in his story was writing about a man at an ayahuasca retreat as well.

Day Nine

The last full day, the crows of roosters, and he was wide awake. Today, Don Pedro was showing them around the farm, which was a much larger affair than the retreat. Daniel skipped breakfast, feeling a bit bloated, and arrived at nine for the tour. As a group, they followed Don Pedro into a fenced area where various herbs and jungle plants used for medicine were growing. There was the piñon colorado, which they had used in the purging ceremony, and other plants. Next, they visited an area used to make mulch, and the mulch indeed was very black and loamy. They crossed the dirt road, and Daniel recognized small cacao trees, the weird bubbly pods. The farm was quite large, but the tour was limited to about forty-five minutes, and soon they were back. Daniel hoped there would not be a group circle, but there was, and those who had taken the optional ceremony glowed, sharing their visions and light shows. Once over, Daniel retreated to his tambo, thoroughly tired and ready for a nap. Whereas he'd had diarrhea the first few days, now he was constipated.

Day Ten

The night before, Daniel packed. He'd left his rain boots and a few other items, which he would not need.

He was ready to go and could already feel himself on the plane, looking down at the jungle.

He poured the last of the water into the toilet, flushing it for the final time, then hefted his heavy backpack. Others were already gathered, and he'd missed breakfast. With the backpacks loaded onto a moto, the group said their goodbyes to Don Pedro and the staff of Pitarika. Down the dirt road they went, passing the occasional house, and soon arrived in Manacamiri. They meandered down to the Nanay River across a muddy slope and navigated a narrow board into the long, colorful wooden boat, their backpacks already loaded. The boat ride was slow and pleasant with a slight breeze on the crooked river. Although he could not blame Don Pedro for not doing his best (he sang for nearly five hours straight after all), Daniel was sad that he had not had any visions. He thought about the story he was writing, how the man in the story had made crazy new friends, had swum with piranhas (no one would really know, right?), and was ready to see his daughters, Samantha and Chelsea, and tell them all about it.

www.ingramcontent.com/pod-product-compliance
Lightning Source LLC
Chambersburg PA
CBHW032043180726
48284CB00008B/2736